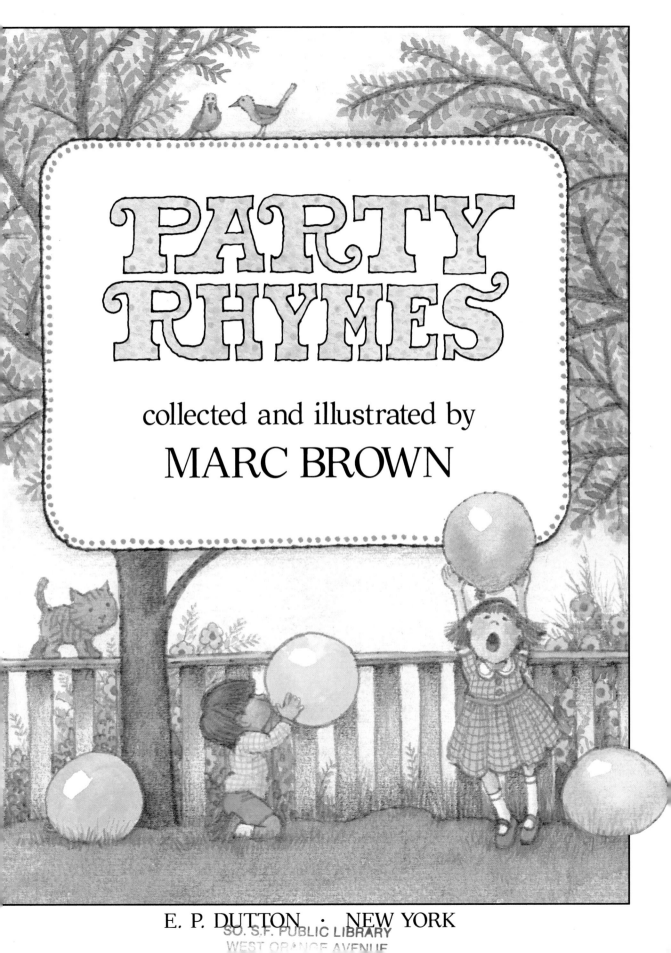

PARTY RHYMES

collected and illustrated by

MARC BROWN

E. P. DUTTON · NEW YORK

Throughout this book,
the circles in the pictograms
represent children forming a circle.

The copyright, CIP data,
and music arrangement
permissions are on page 48.

Contents

The Farmer in the Dell

The farmer in the dell,
The farmer in the dell,
Hi ho, the derrio,
The farmer in the dell.

The farmer takes a wife,
The farmer takes a wife,
Hi ho, the derrio,
The farmer takes a wife.

The wife takes a child,
The wife takes a child,
Hi ho, the derrio,
The wife takes a child.

The child takes a nurse,
The child takes a nurse,
Hi ho, the derrio,
The child takes a nurse.

Form a circle around the farmer. Each
player chosen joins the farmer in the center
while the rest skip around them. Before
last verse, all but cheese rejoin the circle.

(Music is on page 40.) 5

The nurse takes a dog,
The nurse takes a dog,
Hi ho, the derrio,
The nurse takes a dog.

The dog takes a cat,
The dog takes a cat,
Hi ho, the derrio,
The dog takes a cat.

The cat takes a rat,
The cat takes a rat,
Hi ho, the derrio,
The cat takes a rat.

The rat takes a cheese,
The rat takes a cheese,
Hi ho, the derrio,
The rat takes a cheese.

The cheese stands alone,
The cheese stands alone,
Hi ho, the derrio,
The cheese stands alone.

Here We Go Round the Mulberry Bush

Here we go round the mulberry bush,
Mulberry bush, mulberry bush.
Here we go round the mulberry bush,
Early in the morning.

This is the way we wash our clothes,
Wash our clothes, wash our clothes.
This is the way we wash our clothes,
Early Monday morning.

This is the way we iron our clothes,
Iron our clothes, iron our clothes.
This is the way we iron our clothes,
Early Tuesday morning.

Skip in a circle, holding hands, during the first and
last verses. Act out the other verses as shown.

(Music is on page 41.)   9

This is the way we scrub the floor,
Scrub the floor, scrub the floor.
This is the way we scrub the floor,
Early Wednesday morning.

This is the way we mend our clothes,
Mend our clothes, mend our clothes.
This is the way we mend our clothes,
Early Thursday morning.

This is the way we sweep the house,
Sweep the house, sweep the house.
This is the way we sweep the house,
Early Friday morning.

And now we play when work is done,
Work is done, work is done.
And now we play when work is done,
Early Saturday morning.

A-tisket, A-tasket

A-tisket, A-tasket,
A green and yellow basket,
I sent a letter to my friend,
And on the way I dropped it.

I dropped it, I dropped it,
And on the way I dropped it,
A little boy, he came along,
And put it in his pocket.

Hold hands in a circle. One player skips around outside the circle with a handkerchief. She drops it behind another player and then races around the circle while the chosen player races in the other direction. The first to get back to the empty space joins the circle. The other player picks up the handkerchief, and the game starts over.

In and Out the Window

Go round and round the village,
Go round and round the village,
Go round and round the village,
As we have done before.

Go in and out the window,
Go in and out the window,
Go in and out the window,
As we have done before.

Hold hands in a circle. One player skips around outside the circle during the first verse. This player goes in and out under the upraised arms in Verse 2, picks a partner in Verse 3, and leads him as shown in Verses 4 and 5. In Verse 6, the partner becomes the player outside the circle, and the game is repeated.

(Music is on page 42.) 15

Now go and pick a partner,
Now bow before your partner,
Now swing your brand-new partner,
As we have done before.

Now follow me to Boston,
Now follow me to Boston,
Now follow me to Boston,
As we have done before.

Go in and out the window,
Go in and out the window,
Go in and out the window,
As we have done before.

Now run and leave your partner,
Now run and leave your partner,
Now run and leave your partner,
As we have done before.

London Bridge Is Falling Down

London Bridge is falling down,
Falling down, falling down.
London Bridge is falling down,
My fair lady.

Move in a circle under the upraised arms of two players,
who form an arch. At the words *My fair lady*, the arms
drop, catching a player who then stands aside. Repeat till
all have been caught.

(Music is on page 43.)

Build it up with sticks and stones,
Sticks and stones, sticks and stones.
Build it up with sticks and stones,
My fair lady.

Sticks and stones will fall away,
Fall away, fall away.
Sticks and stones will fall away,
My fair lady.

Build it up with iron bars,
Iron bars, iron bars.
Build it up with iron bars,
My fair lady.

Iron bars will bend and break,
Bend and break, bend and break.
Iron bars will bend and break,
My fair lady.

Build it up with pins and needles,
Pins and needles, pins and needles.
Build it up with pins and needles,
My fair lady.

Pins and needles will rust and break,
Rust and break, rust and break.
Pins and needles will rust and break,
My fair lady.

Take a key and lock her up,
Lock her up, lock her up.
Take a key and lock her up,
My fair lady.

Pawpaw Patch

Where oh where is pretty little Sally?
Where oh where is pretty little Sally?
Where oh where is pretty little Sally?
Way down yonder in the pawpaw patch.

Come on, boys, let's go find her.
Come on, boys, let's go find her.
Come on, boys, let's go find her
Way down yonder in the pawpaw patch.

Picking up pawpaws, put 'em in your pocket.
Picking up pawpaws, put 'em in your pocket.
Picking up pawpaws, put 'em in your pocket
Way down yonder in the pawpaw patch.

Hold her tight, so you won't lose her.
Hold her tight, so you won't lose her.
Hold her tight, so you won't lose her
Way down yonder in the pawpaw patch.

Form a circle and stand with eyes covered. One player skips off and
hides nearby. At the words *Come on, boys*, the rest skip off to find her.
Repeat the second verse until she is found. Then sing on, pretending to
pick up pawpaws. At the words *Hold her tight*, join hands in a circle
around Sally, and return her to the starting place.

Fox in a Box

A-hunting we will go,
A-hunting we will go.

We'll catch a fox
And put him in a box,

And then we'll let him go.

(Music is on page 44.)

Skip in a circle, holding hands. One player skips around outside the circle in the other direction. At the words *We'll catch*, the two players nearest the fox raise their clasped hands and bring them down around him, pulling him into the circle. At the words *let him go*, the players holding the fox raise their clasped hands and let him out of the circle. He picks a new fox. The game starts over.

Skip to My Lou

Lost my partner, what'll I do?
Lost my partner, what'll I do?
Lost my partner, what'll I do?
Skip to my lou, my darling.

I'll get another one, prettier than you.
I'll get another one, prettier than you.
I'll get another one, prettier than you.
Skip to my lou, my darling.

Flies in the dairy, shoo, fly, shoo.
Flies in the dairy, shoo, fly, shoo.
Flies in the dairy, shoo, fly, shoo.
Skip to my lou, my darling.

Stand with partners in a circle. One player skips around outside the circle. At the words *I'll get another one*, he chooses someone. They skip around the outside together. Then they join the circle, and all act out the words as shown. When the game starts over, the one whose partner was chosen is the skipper.

(Music is on page 45.)   27

Cats in the buttermilk, two by two.
Cats in the buttermilk, two by two.
Cats in the buttermilk, two by two.
Skip to my lou, my darling.

Mice in the bread tray, chew, mice, chew.
Mice in the bread tray, chew, mice, chew.
Mice in the bread tray, chew, mice, chew.
Skip to my lou, my darling.

Roosters on the fence post, cock-a-doodle-doo.
Roosters on the fence post, cock-a-doodle-doo.
Roosters on the fence post, cock-a-doodle-doo.
Skip to my lou, my darling.

Snail

Hand in hand, you see us well
Creep like a snail into his shell,
Ever nearer, ever nearer,
Ever closer, ever closer.
Very snug indeed you dwell,
Snail, within your tiny shell.

Hand in hand, you see us well
Creep like a snail out of his shell.
Ever farther, ever farther,
Ever wider, ever wider.
Who'd have thought this tiny shell
Could have held us all so well?

Form a line, holding hands. During the first verse, the leader winds the line into a spiral. During the second verse, the leader unwinds it.

(Music is on page 47.)

She'll Be Coming Round the Mountain

She'll be coming round the mountain when she comes.

She'll be coming round the mountain when she comes.

She'll be coming round the mountain,

She'll be coming round the mountain,

She'll be coming round the mountain

   when she comes.

Toot, toot!

She'll be driving six white horses when she comes.

She'll be driving six white horses when she comes.

She'll be driving six white horses,

She'll be driving six white horses,

She'll be driving six white horses

   when she comes.

Whoa, back! Toot, toot!

Form a circle and sing the verses. Shout the
words in italics, and act them out as shown.
Repeat actions as words are repeated.

(Music is on page 46.) 33

Oh, we'll all go out to meet her when she comes.
Oh, we'll all go out to meet her when she comes.
Oh, we'll all go out to meet her,
Oh, we'll all go out to meet her,
Oh, we'll all go out to meet her
  when she comes.

How do! Whoa, back! Toot, toot!

And we'll all have chicken and dumplings when she comes.
And we'll all have chicken and dumplings when she comes.
And we'll all have chicken and dumplings,
And we'll all have chicken and dumplings,
And we'll all have chicken and dumplings
  when she comes.

Yum, yum! How do! Whoa, back! Toot, toot!

She'll be wearing red pajamas when she comes.

She'll be wearing red pajamas when she comes.

She'll be wearing red pajamas,

She'll be wearing red pajamas,

She'll be wearing red pajamas

   when she comes.

Scratch, scratch!

Yum, yum!

How do!

Whoa, back!

Toot, toot!

Me and My Horse

Me and my horse go hippity-hoppity.

Me and my horse go clippity-cloppity,

As we go riding jiggity-joggity,

Over the rolling plain.

It is spring, the daisies are popping out.

It is spring, the grass is tender,

As we go riding jiggity-joggity,

Over the rolling plain.

Form a circle in pairs of horse (in front) and rider (behind) as shown. Gallop in a circle. When the second verse begins, the horses bend to eat grass. At the words *As we go riding,* all circle again. Players reverse roles, and the game starts over.

(Music is on page 47.)

The Muffin Man

Oh, have you seen the muffin man,
The muffin man, the muffin man?
Oh, have you seen the muffin man
Who lives in Drury Lane, O?

Oh yes, I've seen the muffin man,
The muffin man, the muffin man.
Oh yes, I've seen the muffin man
Who lives in Drury Lane, O!

Move in a circle slowly, holding hands. One player, blind-folded, stands in the middle and points to someone who becomes the Muffin Man. During the second verse, the circle dances around them. When the game starts over, the Muffin Man becomes the blindfolded player.

(Music is on page 42.)

The Farmer in the Dell

The far-mer in the dell,— The far-mer in the dell,—

Hi ho, the der-ri-o, The far-mer in the dell.—

The farmer takes a wife,	The dog takes a cat,
The farmer takes a wife,	The dog takes a cat,
Hi ho, the derrio,	Hi ho, the derrio,
The farmer takes a wife.	The dog takes a cat.
The wife takes a child,	The cat takes a rat,
The wife takes a child,	The cat takes a rat,
Hi ho, the derrio,	Hi ho, the derrio,
The wife takes a child.	The cat takes a rat.
The child takes a nurse,	The rat takes a cheese,
The child takes a nurse,	The rat takes a cheese,
Hi ho, the derrio,	Hi ho, the derrio,
The child takes a nurse.	The rat takes a cheese.
The nurse takes a dog,	The cheese stands alone,
The nurse takes a dog,	The cheese stands alone,
Hi ho, the derrio,	Hi ho, the derrio,
The nurse takes a dog.	The cheese stands alone.

Here We Go Round the Mulberry Bush

Here we go round the mul - ber - ry bush, Mul - ber - ry bush, mul - ber - ry bush.

Here we go round the mul - ber - ry bush, Ear - ly in— the mor - ning.

This is the way we wash our clothes,
Wash our clothes, wash our clothes.
This is the way we wash our clothes,
Early Monday morning.

This is the way we iron our clothes,
Iron our clothes, iron our clothes.
This is the way we iron our clothes,
Early Tuesday morning.

This is the way we scrub the floor,
Scrub the floor, scrub the floor.
This is the way we scrub the floor,
Early Wednesday morning.

This is the way we mend our clothes,
Mend our clothes, mend our clothes.
This is the way we mend our clothes,
Early Thursday morning.

This is the way we sweep the house,
Sweep the house, sweep the house.
This is the way we sweep the house,
Early Friday morning.

And now we play when work is done,
Work is done, work is done.
And now we play when work is done,
Early Saturday morning.

A-tisket, A-tasket

A - tis - ket, A - tas - ket, A green and yel - low bas - ket, I

sent a let - ter to my friend, And on the way I dropped it.

I dropped it, I dropped it,
And on the way I dropped it,

A little boy, he came along,
And put it in his pocket.

In and Out the Window

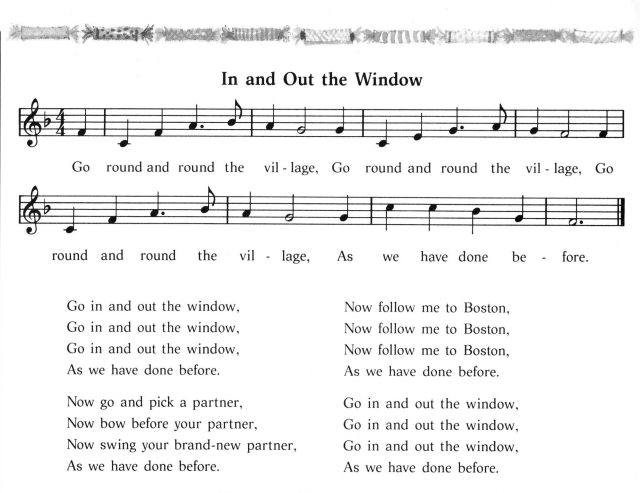

Go round and round the vil - lage, Go round and round the vil - lage, Go

round and round the vil - lage, As we have done be - fore.

Go in and out the window,
Go in and out the window,
Go in and out the window,
As we have done before.

Now go and pick a partner,
Now bow before your partner,
Now swing your brand-new partner,
As we have done before.

Now follow me to Boston,
Now follow me to Boston,
Now follow me to Boston,
As we have done before.

Go in and out the window,
Go in and out the window,
Go in and out the window,
As we have done before.

Now run and leave your partner,
Now run and leave your partner,
Now run and leave your partner,
As we have done before.

The Muffin Man

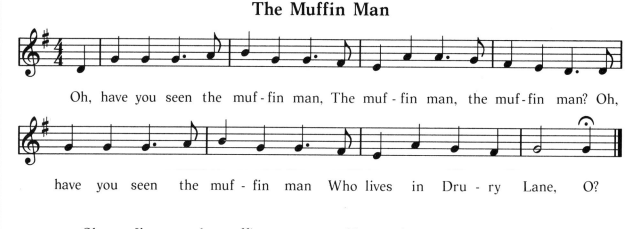

Oh, have you seen the muf - fin man, The muf - fin man, the muf - fin man? Oh,

have you seen the muf - fin man Who lives in Dru - ry Lane, O?

Oh yes, I've seen the muffin man,
The muffin man, the muffin man.

Oh yes, I've seen the muffin man
Who lives in Drury Lane, O!

London Bridge Is Falling Down

Lon - don Bridge is   fall - ing down,   Fall - ing down,   fall - ing down.

Lon - don Bridge is   fall - ing down,   My   fair   la - dy.

Build it up with sticks and stones,
Sticks and stones, sticks and stones.
Build it up with sticks and stones,
My fair lady.

Sticks and stones will fall away,
Fall away, fall away.
Sticks and stones will fall away,
My fair lady.

Build it up with iron bars,
Iron bars, iron bars.
Build it up with iron bars,
My fair lady.

Iron bars will bend and break,
Bend and break, bend and break.
Iron bars will bend and break,
My fair lady.

Build it up with pins and needles,
Pins and needles, pins and needles.
Build it up with pins and needles,
My fair lady.

Pins and needles will rust and break,
Rust and break, rust and break.
Pins and needles will rust and break,
My fair lady.

Take a key and lock her up,
Lock her up, lock her up.
Take a key and lock her up,
My fair lady.

Pawpaw Patch

Where oh where is pret-ty lit-tle Sal-ly? Where oh where is pret-ty lit-tle Sal-ly?

Where oh where is pret-ty lit-tle Sal-ly? Way down yon-der in the paw-paw patch.

Come on, boys, let's go find her.
Come on, boys, let's go find her.
Come on, boys, let's go find her
Way down yonder in the pawpaw patch.

Picking up pawpaws, put 'em in your pocket.　　Hold her tight, so you won't lose her.
Picking up pawpaws, put 'em in your pocket.　　Hold her tight, so you won't lose her.
Picking up pawpaws, put 'em in your pocket　　Hold her tight, so you won't lose her
Way down yonder in the pawpaw patch.　　Way down yonder in the pawpaw patch.

Fox in a Box

A - hunt-ing we will go,—— A - hunt-ing we will go.—— We'll

catch a fox And put him in a box, And then we'll let him go.——

Skip to My Lou

Lost my part-ner, what-'ll I do? Lost my part-ner, what-'ll I do?

Lost my part-ner, what-'ll I do? Skip to my lou, my dar - ling.

I'll get another one, prettier than you.
I'll get another one, prettier than you.
I'll get another one, prettier than you.
Skip to my lou, my darling.

Cats in the buttermilk, two by two.
Cats in the buttermilk, two by two.
Cats in the buttermilk, two by two.
Skip to my lou, my darling.

Flies in the dairy, shoo, fly, shoo.
Flies in the dairy, shoo, fly, shoo.
Flies in the dairy, shoo, fly, shoo.
Skip to my lou, my darling.

Mice in the bread tray, chew, mice, chew.
Mice in the bread tray, chew, mice, chew.
Mice in the bread tray, chew, mice, chew.
Skip to my lou, my darling.

Roosters on the fence post, cock-a-doodle-doo.
Roosters on the fence post, cock-a-doodle-doo.
Roosters on the fence post, cock-a-doodle-doo.
Skip to my lou, my darling.

She'll Be Coming Round the Mountain

She'll be com - ing round the moun - tain when she comes.

She'll be com - ing round the moun - tain when she comes.

She'll be com - ing round the moun-tain, She'll be com - ing round the

moun-tain, She'll be com - ing round the moun-tain when she comes. *Toot,* *toot!*

She'll be driving six white horses
    when she comes.
She'll be driving six white horses
    when she comes.
She'll be driving six white horses,
She'll be driving six white horses,
She'll be driving six white horses
    when she comes.
Whoa, back! Toot, toot!

Oh, we'll all go out to meet her
    when she comes.
Oh, we'll all go out to meet her
    when she comes.
Oh, we'll all go out to meet her,
Oh, we'll all go out to meet her,
Oh, we'll all go out to meet her
    when she comes.
How do! Whoa, back!
Toot, toot!

And we'll all have chicken and dumplings
    when she comes.
And we'll all have chicken and dumplings
    when she comes.
And we'll all have chicken and dumplings,
And we'll all have chicken and dumplings,
And we'll all have chicken and dumplings
    when she comes.
Yum, yum! How do! Whoa, back! Toot, toot!

She'll be wearing red pajamas
    when she comes.
She'll be wearing red pajamas
    when she comes.
She'll be wearing red pajamas,
She'll be wearing red pajamas,
She'll be wearing red pajamas
    when she comes.
Scratch, scratch! Yum, yum! How do!
Whoa, back! Toot, toot!

Snail

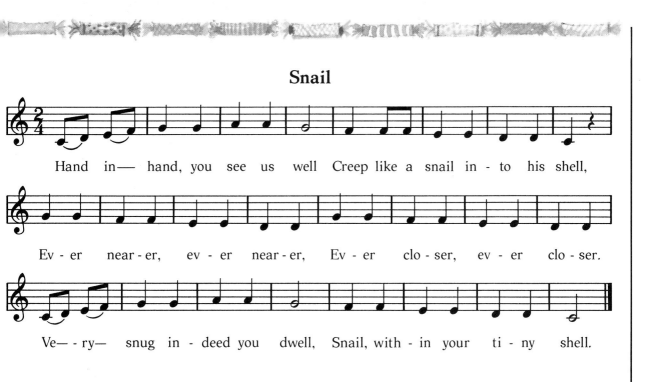

Hand in— hand, you see us well Creep like a snail in-to his shell,

Ev - er near-er, ev - er near-er, Ev - er clo - ser, ev - er clo - ser.

Ve—-ry— snug in - deed you dwell, Snail, with - in your ti - ny shell.

Hand in hand, you see us well
Creep like a snail out of his shell.
Ever farther, ever farther,

Ever wider, ever wider.
Who'd have thought this tiny shell
Could have held us all so well?

Me and My Horse

Me and my horse go hip-pi-ty-hop-pi-ty. Me and my horse go clip-pi-ty-clop-pi-ty,

As we go ri - ding jig - gi - ty - jog - gi - ty, o - ver the roll—-ing plain.

It is spring, the daisies are popping out.
It is spring, the grass is tender,

As we go riding jiggity-joggity,
Over the rolling plain.

LAURIE, YOU ARE MY PARTY PARTNER.
M.

Published in the United States by E. P. Dutton,
2 Park Avenue, New York, N.Y. 10016,
a division of NAL Penguin Inc.

Published simultaneously in Canada by
Fitzhenry & Whiteside Limited, Toronto

Editor: Ann Durell

Printed in the U.S.A.
First Edition   COBE   10 9 8 7 6 5 4 3 2 1

Library of Congress Cataloging-in-Publication Data

Party rhymes/collected and illustrated by Marc Brown.—1st ed.
    p.   cm.
    Summary: A collection of twelve play rhymes with illustrations to
demonstrate the accompanying finger plays or physical activities.
Includes music for the rhymes which are also songs.
    ISBN 0-525-44402-5
    1. Circle games—Juvenile literature.   2. Nursery rhymes—Juvenile
literature.   3. Songs—Juvenile literature.   4. Singing games—
Juvenile literature.   [1. Circle games.   2. Nursery rhymes.
3. Songs.]   I. Brown, Marc Tolon.   88-17680
GV1218.C47P37   1988   CIP
793.4—dc19   AC

The author and publisher gratefully acknowledge permission to reprint the music ar-
rangements on:

    pages 40, 42 *top*, and 43–46, by permission of Sterling Publishing Co., Inc., Two
Park Avenue, New York, NY 10016, from *The Best Singing Games for Children of All
Ages* by Edgar S. Bley, © 1957 by Sterling Publishing Co., Inc.

    page 47 *bottom*, by permission of Sterling Publishing Co., Inc., Two Park Avenue, New
York, NY 10016, from *Musical Games for Children of All Ages* by Esther L. Nelson, © 1976
by Esther L. Nelson.

    pages 41 *top*, 42 *bottom*, and 47 *top*, with permission of Macmillan Publishing Com-
pany from *Games* by Jesse H. Bancroft. Copyright 1937 by Macmillan Publishing Com-
pany, renewed 1965 by Mrs. Earl A. Aldrich.

    page 41 *bottom*, from *Do Your Ears Hang Low? 50 More Musical Fingerplays* by Tom
Glazer; Doubleday & Co., New York, NY. © Songs Music, Inc., Scarborough, NY 10510.
By Permission.